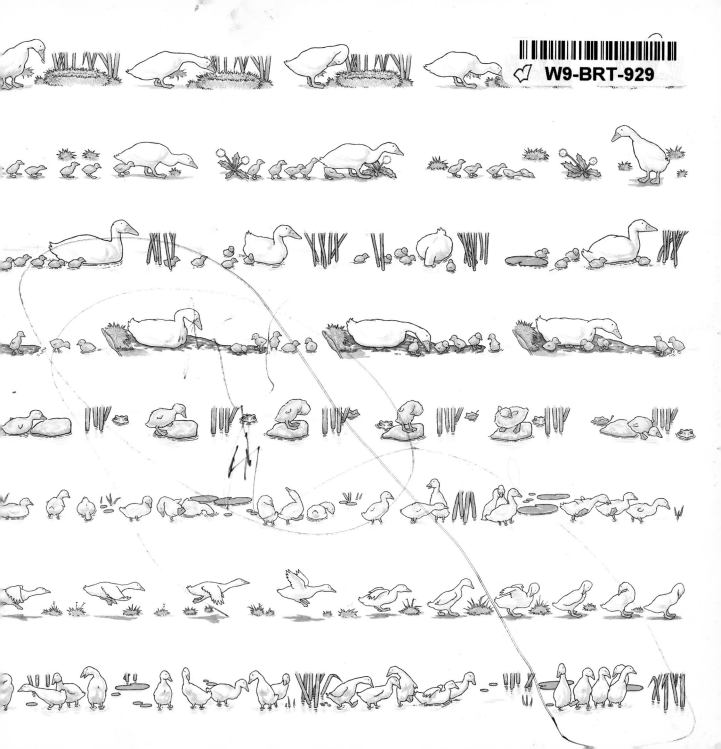

CREATED BY DORLING KINDERSLEY

Library of Congress Cataloging-in-Publication Data

Watts, Barrie.
  Duck/photographed by Barrie Watts.—1st American ed.
   p. cm.—(See how they grow)
  Summary: Photographs and text show the development of a duck from
the egg stage through six weeks old.
  ISBN 0–525–67346–6
  1. Duck—Juvenile literature. 2. Duck—Development—Juvenile
literature. [1. Duck. 2. Animals—Infancy.]
I. Title. II. Series.
QL696.A52W39 1991
598.4'1—dc20
                                                90–13536
                                                     CIP
                                                     AC

First published in the United States in 1991 by Lodestar Books,
an affiliate of Dutton Children's Books, a division of
Penguin Books USA Inc.

Originally published in Great Britain in 1991 by
Dorling Kindersley Limited, 9 Henrietta Street, London WC2E 8PS

Printed in Italy by L.E.G.O.   ISBN 0–525–67346–6
First American Edition   10 9 8 7 6 5 4 3 2 1

Written and edited by Angela Royston
Art Editor Nigel Hazle
Illustrator Rowan Clifford

Typesetting by Goodfellow & Egan
Color reproduction by Scantrans, Singapore

DUCK

photographed by
BARRIE WATTS

Lodestar Books • Dutton • New York

In the nest

My mother has laid her eggs in this nest. She sits on them to keep them warm.

Inside each egg a new duckling is growing. This one is me. I am just beginning to hatch.

Just hatched

I have chipped
away my shell,
and now I am
pushing myself out.

At last I am out of my shell.

I can see, hear, stand, and walk.
I can cheep too. Where
is my mother?

First swim

I am two days old now. I am going to the pond for my first swim.

As soon as I am in the water, I start to swim.

I use my webbed feet to
paddle through the water.

Feeding

I am one week old and getting bigger. I like to explore everything.

This bowl has wet mud in it.
I search the mud with my
beak for things to eat.

Look! I've jumped right into the bowl.

In the water

I look for
things to
eat on the
surface.

I am two weeks old,
and I love to swim
in the water.

I shake the water off my body.

New feathers

I am three weeks old.
My yellow down is
falling out, and new
white feathers are
beginning to grow.

I stay close to the other ducklings.
Our mother watches out for danger.

Sometimes we huddle
together. Our feathers help
to keep us warm.

Nearly grown up

I am six weeks old and nearly
grown up.

All my feathers are white, and my wings are big and strong.

See how much I have grown. This bowl is small, but it seemed big when I first jumped into it.

See how I grew

The egg

One hour old

Two days old

Seven days old

Two weeks old

Three weeks old   Six weeks old

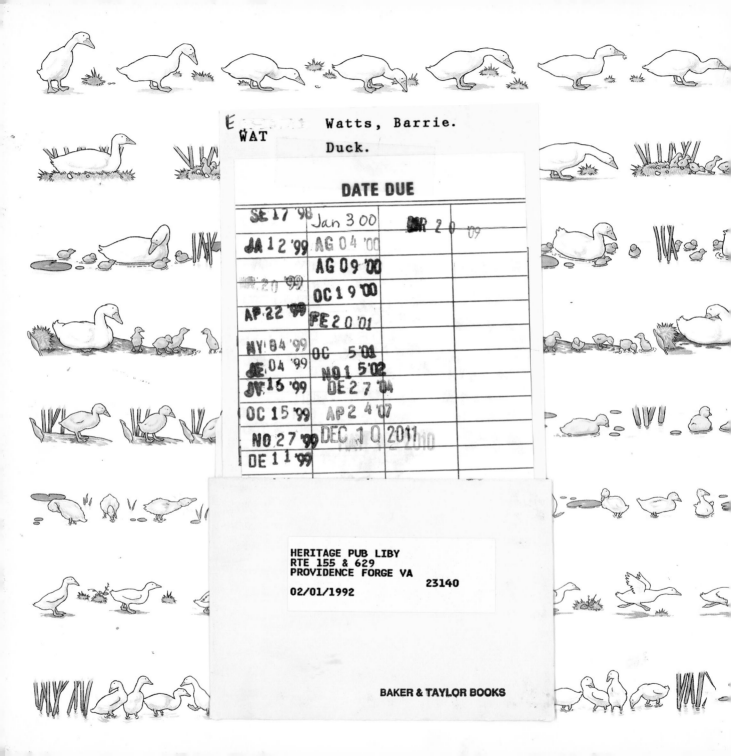

E   Watts, Barrie.
WAT   Duck.

DATE DUE

SE 17 '98	Jan 3 00	MR 20 09	
JA 12 '99	AG 04 '00		
	AG 09 '00		
MR 20 '99	OC 19 '00		
AP 22 '99	FE 20 '01		
MY 04 '99	OC 5 '01		
JE 04 '99	NO 15 '02		
JY 16 '99	DE 27 '04		
OC 15 '99	AP 2 4 07		
NO 27 '99	DEC 1 0 2011		
DE 11 '99			